AND I
MEAN IT,
STANLEY

Weekly Reader Books presents

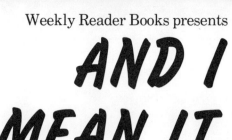

AND I MEAN IT, STANLEY

by Crosby Bonsall

An EARLY I CAN READ Book

Harper & Row, Publishers
New York, Evanston, San Francisco, London

This book is a presentation of Weekly Reader Books.
Weekly Reader Books offers book clubs for children from
preschool through junior high school.

For further information write to:
Weekly Reader Books
1250 Fairwood Ave.
Columbus, Ohio 43216

AND I MEAN IT, STANLEY

Copyright © 1974 by Crosby Bonsall

Library of Congress Catalog Card Number: 73–14324
Trade Standard Book Number: 06–020567–9
Harpercrest Standard Book Number: 06–020568–7

This book
is for
SUSAN And PAUL
HIRSCHPERSON

Listen, Stanley.

I know you are there.

I know you are

in back of the fence.

But I don't care, Stanley.

I don't want to play with you.

I don't want to talk to you.

You stay there, Stanley.

Stay in back of the fence.

I don't care.

I can play by myself, Stanley.

I don't need you, Stanley.

And I mean it, Stanley.

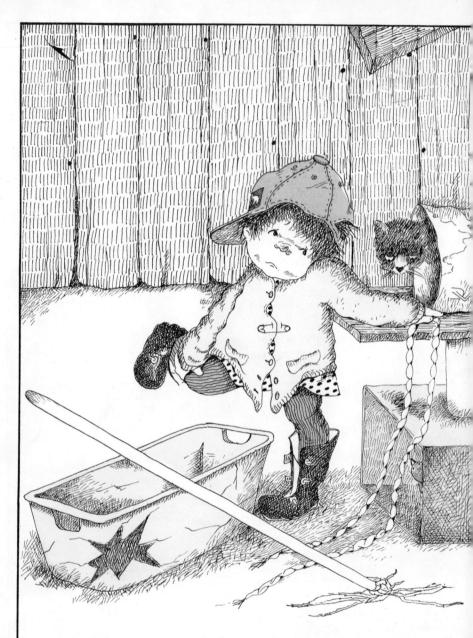

I am having a lot of fun.

A lot of fun!

I am making a great thing, Stanley.

A really, truly great thing.

And when it is done,

you will want to see it, Stanley.

Well, you can't.

I don't want you to.

And I mean it, Stanley.

I don't want you to see

what I am making.

You stay there, Stanley.

Don't you look.

Don't you look.

Don't even peek.

You hear me, Stanley?

This thing I am making

is really neat.

It is really neat, Stanley.

And it is all made now.

The very best thing I ever made.

But don't you look, Stanley.

I don't want you to see it.

And I mean it. . .

STANLEY!

Aw, Stanley.